T0068226

The Insect Vegetable Wars

RAYMOND C. WOOD

iUniverse

THE INSECT VEGETABLE WARS

iUniverse books may be ordered through booksellers or by contacting:

iUniverse
1663 Liberty Drive
Bloomington, IN 47403
www.iuniverse.com
844-349-9409

Because of the dynamic nature of the Internet, any web addresses or links contained in this book may have changed since publication and may no longer be valid. The views expressed in this work are solely those of the author and do not necessarily reflect the views of the publisher, and the publisher hereby disclaims any responsibility for them.

Any people depicted in stock imagery provided by Getty Images are models, and such images are being used for illustrative purposes only. Certain stock imagery © Getty Images.

ISBN: 978-1-6632-5982-0 (sc)
ISBN: 978-1-6632-5983-7 (e)

Library of Congress Control Number: 2024901068

Print information available on the last page.

iUniverse rev. date: 01/12/2024

Preface

This is Ray's third book in a trilogy of witchcraft, following *Underneath Rockville* and *Baby's Sofia's Reckoning*.

Satan unleashes millions of rogue insects and vegetables to tear into humankind, spreading deadly diseases in an intense chess match with God, as He counters with an army of praying mantises. As the battle between good and evil rages on, who will maintain control over human souls?

And yes, Lyla, you did hear voices
underneath the vegetable garden!

Chapter One

I T HAS BEEN THREE YEARS since the crazy turn of events that shook up the small town of Rockville, MA, where carpenter, Shawn Ross, was found dead on the riverbanks, apparently having been stung to death by hornets, bees, wasps, or some combination of the three. The police chief and his officers hadn't been able to locate any nests in the area. After an exhausting search for themselves, Mark and Billy, the twin Martin brothers and former coworkers of the deceased, were unable to find any evidence that matched what the medical examiner had concluded. The bizarre death of their friend followed on the heels of the twins near deadly encounters with a crime syndicate, witchcraft, and devil-worshipers.

Since the appalling and unexpected discovery of her husband's death, Shawn's wife, Kim, had fallen into a deep-rooted depression. Unable to cope, she has been frequently admitted to a trauma center, where two doctors and a psychiatrist have been closely treating her shock and trauma.

All three have agreed that such a profound devastation has left Kim's memory rattled and full of inconsistencies, most of the time making very little sense.

After these events unfolded, Mark married a native of Peru, who, as a teen, practiced witchcraft and found that wasn't truly who she was. Mark's twin, Billy, who was party to the full drama only six months prior, married his longtime girlfriend, Cindy Lue. Of course, the twins wanted to talk to Kim and check in on her, but her mother and brother, Kevin, believed it might drudge up memories, doing more harm than good, and be too much for Kim to handle just yet. It would be better, they suggested, for the twins to give her more time to recover, if she does recover…

At the present, the town of Rockville had purchased an abandoned 19th century farm with a reputation for its giant vegetable garden and later, in the 1920's, for producing well-trained, winning racehorses. The farmhouse was in dire disrepair. Being union carpenters, the twins had been without work for some time as the job market slowed significantly. Wanting to support itself from within, the town hired the twins to renovate the old farmhouse, hoping to breathe new life into the town with its restoration.

The Martin twins were not working alone on such a large job; a third carpenter was hired to work with them on the project. Apprentice Lyla Cody, a tried and tested carpenter already in the brief time she had worked in the industry, was a Jill-of-all-Trades, having honed her skills while working in her father's metal shop just north of Rockville. Standing 5'4" with short, light red hair, she walked over to meet the twins.

Lyla said, as she approached the twins assessing the repairs,

"Hi, guys! I'm Lyla."

"Yeah, we heard you were coming over. I'm Mark and he," pointing to his brother, "is Billy, the two minutes younger brother." Mark laughed as he punched him in the arm.

Billy jostled him right back.

"Yeah, two minutes later but still a year smarter."

Lyla chuckled.

Finally, Mark said, "Lyla, heights don't bother you, do they?"

"Actually, they don't; however, my husband isn't too fond of climbing."

"Well," Billy said, "we have been using a Bosun chair by the peaks. The manager, Alvin Butler, said he's impressed by the architecture of the twin spirals and it would surely be an enhancement for the town."

Besides the carpenters, the job-site also employed laborers, electricians, plumbers, and a few others who would work to bring the farmhouse back to her former glory. After several weeks of working together, the twins and Lyla were taking an afternoon break on one of the high overlooks when eyed the old garden.

"Guys, do you think that the old garden would still have some good soil? My husband wants to start a small tomato patch in the yard and all we have is dust."

Mark donned his shades, saying, "I would say, as long as you dig down a bit, the top soil looks pretty much parched."

"Do you think they would mind if I took a few buckets?"

Billy quipped, "No, of course not. Not unless you find a stash of rubies!"

Lyla laughed. "I don't think there's much chance of that happening."

Chapter Two

A COUPLE OF DAYS LATER DURING another break, Lyla mentioned that she got the loam all spread for the tomato patch and it really jump-started her husband's tomato garden.

"Boys, I'll bring you some when they get ripe!"

Billy smiled, "That's super! Garden tomatoes with a little salt…my wife, Cindy Lue, would be in seventh heaven!" Then adding after a moment, "Lyla, is Cody your husband's name?"

Lyla laughed. "No, Billy! It's my name, but I know what you're going to ask next. Am I related to Buffalo Bill Cody? Well, I am twelve or thirteen times removed, so technically. I told my husband I've always felt women should be able to keep their maiden name and he was completely cool with it."

Giggling, Lyla added, "I've been asked that quite a few times, especially after that play, *Annie Get Your Gun*. Of course, I do have questions about Cody's slaughtering all those buffalo."

"Well," Billy smiled, "I don't know about that, but I am an old western fan. Love the old west. My uncle Jess got me into it when I was a kid with some old tapes of cowboy shows on TV – *Gunsmoke, The Restless Gun, Have a Gun Will Travel* – plenty of others.

Mark chimed in, "God those titles would be toxic today; anything to do with firearms has the left wing saying 'God, country, and guns' in a put down of the Second Amendment.

"Yeah," Lyla responded, "that's why I own a rifle and a .32."

Chapter Three

ABOUT A WEEK LATER, LYLA'S husband decided to expand his garden and asked if she could get more of the rich soil. So, one afternoon under the heat of the June sun, Lyla went to another area of the vast garden to dig when she noted an animal burrow in a small hill adjacent to the garden. As she started to dig, she thought she heard voices coming from beneath the ground or perhaps in the burrow.

The next day, the job supervisor instructed Lyla to team up with Percy Carlton, an electrician, to help him snaking lines by widening existing holes or making new ones for the wiring to go through. Lyla immediately took a liking to the electrician, a dark-skinned man in his late 50's.

At lunch, Percy and Lyla were eating their sandwiches when Lyla decided to tell him about the voices she had heard while digging loam.

Percy smiled. "Maybe the wind was blowing the voices from the house over yonder to where you were."

Lyla laughed. "That's a funny way to describe it. Perhaps

you're right... But I could swear it was coming from right underneath the ground where I was standing."

Percy rubbed his chin and said, "Kiddo, maybe it was a radio from somewhere."

"I don't know, it just spooked me a little."

Percy looked out over to the garden. "Lyla, now you got me wondering."

The following week, Lyla was back working with the Martin twins. At coffee break, she mentioned it to them as well.

Mark said, "Are you sure it wasn't a cell phone somewhere or something?"

"I don't know... I kind of thought all the workers had left. This was at five; you know everybody here clears out at 4:30.

Chapter Four

THE NEXT NIGHT UNDER THE vaults, deep in the underground, a cabal of evil was festering as a giant wood tick called Roman and his surrogates formed an alliance between rogue insects and vegetables. On this night, they were paying homage to the brown, Lima, and pinto beans who killed a human a few years back. Roman was presiding over squads of hostile beans, horseflies, red ants, and termites as well as corn, rhubarb, and onions. Roman called the meeting to begin enacting his grand plan to get his soldiers to kill all the human beings.

"Welcome, friends! Insects! And vegetables! We come here tonight to pin medals on the bevy of beans that honorably began our crusade. At this moment, we are still lacking many vital insects and vegetables, unwilling to take up the fight."

A giant beetle spoke, "Unfortunately, many vegetables and insects don't want to join because humans have a vast number of weapons and chemicals to do us in!"

"I know, I know..." exclaimed Roman. "However, we have the element of surprise and numerous combatants; soon hopefully even more will join. And of course, the Forces of the Burning Inferno miles under the ground have given us the ability to talk, think, and reason, as well as the cunning necessary to defeat the vile humans."

"Yes, yes," spoke Carle Wiggleham, a red ant. "A few months ago, my family was helping to build a new mound when this murderous human came over and blew poisons onto the adobe. Only my little one, Tony, was able to escape it. I want to annihilate all mankind!"

"It's coming, it's coming!" Roman boomed. "So tonight, I want the leaders of each combat force front and center. Of course, we all know that each of you has been attending the Devil's workshop, presided over by Satan himself. We will begin with the horseflies. Why do you want to kill the humans and what is your plan to do so?"

"I am General Hairface. Why do we want to kill the humans? It's very simple. For thousands of eons, the humans have worked to kill us every moment we were in their presence. They hate flies because we are the insect vultures who eat garbage and dead, rotted bodies. We do so not only to sustain ourselves, but to keep Mother Earth clean. My plan has been implemented. In the Devil's workshop we have been fitted with bubonic plague and will fly out across the Northeast and bite humans at every opportunity. Although our lives are short, believe me, we will make good use of the time we flies are given, focusing our wrath in these pinpoint attacks!"

"Ah! Great!" Roman the wood tick smiled. "What say you, hornets?"

"I am Lieutenant Commander Altla. We have been equipped with fentanyl in our stingers. We hate the humans, for the humans have always come after us! Alas! They will pay heavily!"

"What about you, bedbugs?"

"I am Vlad the Impaler of the Bed Bug Federation. We don't really know why we love feeding on humans, but we love their juicy flesh. It's like filet mignon in its perfection. When they try to exterminate us, we will now be carrying anthrax to do them in We will kill them even as we eat them."

"Very good." Roman chuckled. "What about you, red ants?"

A large red ant stepped forward. "I am Commanding General Hercules. All over the world, humans have been trying to kill us just because we are a threat in their minds. Satan's own demons have fitted us with a strain of COVID-19 a score more lethal than anything they have experienced. We will descend upon the big cities like Boston, Providence, Bangor, and Hartford and bring about further disease to destroy these worthless monsters!"

"Good," Roman voiced. "Of course, we already know what the beans are capable of doing. So then, what is your plan, termites?"

Peewee Senor stepped up. "Yes, we are mostly in rotted wood; however, the Devil and demons came up with a true masterpiece. Inside each of my brothers and sisters is the tiniest bit of gamma radiation, nothing to us, but more than strong enough to kill humans. All I can say is that too many termites die each year from people like the Orkin Man. So, my dear Roman, we are going to change the equation!"

"Very well," a beaming Roman espoused. Then, turning to the vegetables, he said, "What about you, Master Ivan the Terrible corn husker?"

"Yes, Roman. We are ready for this assault on mankind. At first my ancestors welcomed the humans. In South America, the natives first grew us, then brought us farther north. However, after this time period, the humans ABUSED us -- the conditions we are forced to grown in, lack of water, storms and changing weather patters due to their selfishness! So much unnecessary damage caused by mankind's disregard of the planet, so far removed from when the bronze and red men cared for us. Every kernel of corn will be laced with Spanish Influenza, far greater in strength and more lethal than its original pandemic. This variant will kill as many as possible!"

Then Roman lit a small cigarillo. "What say you, Barbosa, Knight of the Round Table of Evil Onions?"

"Roman, we're going to rid this world of the humans. There are too many who don't like us."

Roman laughed. "Yes, Barbosa, I am sure lots of people don't like onions, but—"

Barbosa cut the tick off, saying, "That's excuse enough!"

"Okay," Roman followed, "what is your poison for the humans?"

"Our skins have been immersed in deadly swine flu that will slay the humans when eaten!"

"Awesome." Roman was truly tickled by this. "I now turn to the rhubarb."

"Thank you, Roman, for giving us rhubarb a role in dispatching the awful homo sapiens. I am Johnny Red Stalk, CEO of the Brotherhood of Rhubarb. Our skins have been immersed in an even worse SARS virus that goes hand in hand with the oxalic acid already within us. Of course, the fool humans only want to eat the stalk, but will be killed before they even reach that. Like I said, any human will be laid to waste when they come near, and we will celebrate with trumpets and horns!"

"Why would they come over to the rhubarb en-masse?" Roman asked.

"The leaves will have spearmint flavoring."

Roman laughed. "Aha! Good move! I should point out that we wood ticks will be carrying claymore mines when we bite the humans."

"But Roman," Johnny Red Stalk said, "won't that kill you too?"

"Aye, comrade. But there's not a wood tick alive that wouldn't sacrifice his own life to annihilate the evil humans."

Barbosa yelled, "Bravo! Bravo!" as all the insects and vegetables clapped and cheered.

Chapter Five

As the Devil's creations fawned over the humans' impending doom, unbeknownst to them, deep in the shadows, two praying mantises were lurking and taking it all in. Peter Mantis and his son Rob Roy were shocked at what had been going down.

"Pop," Rob Roy quietly said, "why do they make war on humans and want to kill them?"

Peter looked sternly, saying, "Son, the Devil's wrath is playing big here. This is an evil, Satan-orchestrated cabal that he put together in his leeching plan to destroy God's hold over the humans by having them killed. Then Satan and his demons will burn their souls in the Fires of Hell. He'd be drooling over their agony, knowing God was defeated in this battle and the whole earth was in his diabolical hands."

Rob Roy looked perplexed. "What you're saying is Satan is going to unleash these insects and vegetables to kill mankind?"

"Yes, son. Although the Devil is at work here, God is

working too. I would think God has some plan of retribution though, lad, because you and I can also solve problems, talk and reason and think. You see, son, God knows what Satan is up to; that's why I am pretty sure He has a plan, and we are part of it."

"Really!?" Rob Roy was aghast. Looking to his father, he said, "But Pop, what can we do against an army of insects and vegetables?"

"Don't worry Rob, we will follow the signs. I am sure of it."

Down below, the rally began breaking up as Roman said, "Let us not forget that we are also in the process of adding mosquitoes and fire ants to our plan to exterminate the humans!"

"Yay! Yay!" PeeWee Senor of the termites cried. "I want first crack at the Orkin Man!"

The crowd roared as they dispersed, excitedly reviewing the details of their plans.

Chapter Six

BACK AT BILLY AND CINDY Lue's apartment, Billy was awakened suddenly by a fragrance drifting in under his nose. He sat up, knowing it was Cindy Lue's, as he looked over toward her vanity where she sat doing her makeup.

Billy cracked, "I have been to England, I have been to France, and I see Cindy Lue's pink underpants!"

Cindy spun around. "Oh really, Billy? Now why aren't you getting ready for work?"

Billy chuckled, "Probably because I am so fixated on you."

"Never mind, husband. Start the coffee."

Cindy watched in the mirror as Billy walked over, displayed in all his glory.

"No, Billy," she laughed as she rubbed his penis on her panties, then walked it up her back. "Billy, stop you sex fiend! I've got to get dressed. Now relax that thing and put your pants on."

"Oh, Cindy Lue, do I have to?"

"Yes, my love. We had a marathon two nights ago, you silly man, Now get dressed and get the coffee going."

Billy reluctantly went back to the bed, grabbing his jeans off the floor, then said, "Honey, I got a problem."

As she was fixing her mascara, Cindy said, "And what's that?"

"My member won't cooperate and won't relax enough to let me get my pants on..."

Cindy chimed in, "Billy Boy, get dressed before I come over there and hang weights on it."

Immediately they both cracked up with laughter. Given that kind of motivation, Billy obliged and finally started the coffee.

At the job site, Lyla, Percy Carlton, and Mark were shooting the breeze when Billy finally rolled in around 8a.m.

Mark said, "Billy, the super wants us to start renovating the master bedroom as an office."

Percy and Lyla were working together again snaking lines. Percy asked if she needed more loam for the garden.

"Yes, I am going to grab some after work."

"If you don't mind, I'll go with you and see if I hear anything?"

"Gee, thanks, Percy. You don't mind? Maybe I was just delusional..."

"Oh," Percy quipped, "I don't think so."

Before they knew it, 4:30 rolled around and they headed to the back of the garden. Lyla began digging and filling her bucket as Percy stood, listening for any semblance of voices. Suddenly, Percy rushed over to Lyla where she was bent over digging and frantically began brushing red ants from her back.

"What's wrong?!" Lyla cried.

"Get out of the garden! Red ants everywhere!"

Lyla quickly shed her work vest and shook the ants off.

"Wow!" Percy exclaimed. "There must be a nest somewhere."

"Well, anyhow, I got the bucket full at least."

As they turned to leave, Lyla stopped.

"Wait, Percy, listen. Do you hear voices?"

Percy stood quiet for a long moment before he said, "I heard something. Of course, my hearing isn't top notch…"

Then Lyla looked over by the burrow and commented, "What's that plant I see by the burrow?"

Percy walked over.

"It looks like wild rhubarb, judging by the red stalk. And they thrive in well drained soils. My father had some in his garden. Only the stalks are edible. A seed must have come from the garden. Probably back years past more people used them as a food source."

Turning their backs to the burrow, the rhubarb, and the garden, they got into their vehicles and headed home.

Chapter Seven

UNDER THE GROUND IN ONE of the many interconnected tunnels, Peter Mantis and his son were making their way through a passage when they ran into the tall beetle they had seen earlier at the rally.

Immediately the beetle began to panic. "Oh please, Mantis! I am just walking through! Please don't eat me!"

Peter held up his sharp claw. "No worries; we're friendly. We saw you at the rally."

"Oh, yes, Mr. Mantis. What I saw I didn't like."

"Yeah, I could see that," Peter replied. "By the way, just call me Peter. This is my son, Rob Roy."

"Pleased to meet you both. I am Jake."

Peter added, "Do you think any beetles will join that evil force to kill humans?"

"No, not at all. We beetles may look big, but we only kill to survive."

"That's good news," Peter replied. "My mantises are

forming ranks to go against this terrible, horrendous army of the Devil's own making."

Jake's eyes lit up as he said, "Everybody knows that the praying mantises are above and beyond the most effective fighters of all insects. They call you Kung Fu experts in well-documented battles with even larger foes."

"Yeah," Peter smiled, "we are deadly and measured in every move we make. However, Roman the wood tick and his army of evil make for a formidable foe."

Then, rubbing his shell, Jake thought aloud, "Maybe some of the young beetles can infiltrate and act as spies..."

Peter nodded. "That would be good. Find out. You know where we have our grass fort."

"Will do, fellas, but right now I must be off to help my grandfather, Zeke. His shell seems to be sagging. Of course, it's old age, but I won't tell him that. I'll just give him an old-fashioned back rub."

Peter and his son nodded goodbye to the beetle and continued on their journey home as Rob Roy said, "Pop, you didn't tell me that mantises are preparing for war."

"I don't know for sure, son, but I got a feeling that God in the sky is putting together a vision for what he wants to happen."

Rob Roy was taken aback. "Wow, Pop. That's awesome! Why did the beetle call you a Kung-Fu expert?"

"Because we are, son. Us mantises can whip most insects by our strong claws, quick moves, and stealth. Pound for pound, we are the best. Of course, we are not infallible. Our main concern is the armies of ants. They usually attack with several hundred or even thousand soldiers all at once. No insect could survive that, not even us. You know, Rob

Roy, I think you're old enough to know about the birds and the bees."

Rob Roy's green face turned red.

"I know it's hard to hear about, having lost your mother at such a young age due to that virus, but you must know about the cycle of mating that we mantises go through. You see, son, most animals an insects go through a ritual that is quite unique and yet often very much the same. There are a few, though, where the female eats her mate once the rite is completed. You see, son, it's the way of the mating mantises. When your mother and I mated, I was super careful and made sure I had a way to get away from her, given that she is so much bigger and more powerful. If I hadn't, I would have been lunch."

Rob Roy's mouth hung open. "Pop, you mean Mom was going to eat you?"

"Yes, son. I am sorry I had to tell you, but you're old enough now. We mantises are a proud and unique creature. There are over 2,400 species of us and we are beloved by farmers for being so beneficial to their gardens."

Soon the two mantises entered their home in the grass fort. Immediately upon entering, they could see something substantial was happening. They followed in line and joined the many bedecked mantises that were heading to address the assembly of several hundred of their brethren.

A point mantis introduced the high-standing mantises to the crowd, saying, "Mantises, ladybugs, crickets, and all manner of insects gathered before us – we have gathered because we know a terrible cloud of impending calamity of the Devil's own making has descended upon the insect and vegetable kingdoms alike. We have found out that they have a plan to exterminate all humans in the Northeast, which would surely be a bellwether in this spread of extermination to other states and areas of the world beyond.

Standing here before you are three Generals from the 64th Army Brigade of Southeast Massachusetts. All are seasoned mantises of the quintessential Ripping Shred Crushers Unit. We have Dwight D. Eisenhower, who likes to be called General Ike. He takes his name from the great commander of Allied expeditionary forces in World War II, of course. Next is General George Patton, known as "Old Blood and Guts". And then this is General Charles Martell, who was actually once a duke and is called "The Hammer". His forces defeated a foreign enemy attempting to take over Europe in 714 at the Battle of Tours. Also, our esteemed diplomats, Teddy Roosevelt, a U.S. president whose motto was "Speak softly and carry a big stick", as well as his cousin Franklin Roosevelt, another U.S. president, who led the U.S. through the Great Depression as well as World War II. Beside him you will find Winston Churchill, who was at the helm during World War II as well, and whose famous quotes still ring out, including "All I can offer is blood, toil, tears, and sweat" as well as "Never surrender!". These mantises possess all the most vital traits of their namesakes who lived so long ago. Now, we will let General Ike fill in everyone who has come."

"Thank you, point mantis. Thank you everybody assembled here on this day. Satan and his cohorts of unfathomable evil have what he says is 'a calling' to eradicate the human race, and believe me, I am sure he as formulated a well-devised plan. The real issue here is Satan wants to have possession of their souls so he and his demons can send them to Hell and bask in their terrible screams as they slowly burn within the inferno. Like us, friends, the humans are not perfect, but we must push back or Satan will be the landlord, if you will, to all living things. It has also been discovered that Satan will use millions of the humans as slaves. As you may know, Satan is a big fan of the Egyptian pharaohs of the past, who would work their slaves to death, right up until their very burial."

Then, Ike called to General Patton to respond.

"Thank you, General Ike. We know in just a few days millions of horseflies are going to attack the coastal community of Little John's, RI with the bubonic plague to kill humans indiscriminately. However, my friends, we have a push back of epic proportions. Daddy long legs, the spiders with eight legs, are willing to help us in our need and will team up with the hummingbirds."

The mostly mantis crowd was stunned, one saying, "Spiders and birds together? What?!"

General Patton smiled. "We all know Satan has put together an Axis of Evil. Well, my friends, God also has a trick or two in His repertoire. Daddy long legs are being carried by the hummingbirds. They are constructed huge webs in trees, where these horseflies will surely meet their doom."

The huge crowd let out a loud applause. Then General Patton spoke again.

"It won't be easy in defeating the evil armada. I think it's going to be a chess game between God and Satan."

Chapter Eight

MEANWHILE, IN PARK CITY, MARK and his wife Shara were commenting on how time had flown by since Baby Sofia was now four years old.

Shara then said to Mark, "I noticed the last few days that Sofia seems agitated."

"How's that?"

"I don't know, but she seems like she's trying to process something."

"Really, hon, what, at her age, could she be thinking about? Maybe she's looking for a cookie or something."

Shara went over and got her one, but Sofia ignored it.

Chapter Nine

THE COALITION OF MANTISES FOUND out that a second wave of the Devil's wrath in the form of hornets loaded with fentanyl was getting ready for an assault on Stoneport, MA. General Ike conferred with the other generals and determined that they would intercept them with a special unit of mantises, who were armed with tiny sniper rifles as well as blow guns that would fire balls that quickly metastasized into a cloud of poison. When the results came back, it was said that the hornets were completely wiped out. Although it was a great joy that the fentanyl attack was throttled, Ike knew the Devil would try to even the score.

In the corn fields and at vegetable stands, people unknowingly bought corn whose kernels had been laced with Spanish flu and many died. The governor put out a dire emergency to everybody not to eat corn.

General Patton told the other generals that he should lead a task force to the Devil's compound, which they call Little Hades, and reign his own hell upon them. After much debate, and despite an extremely high risk, they all agreed. Patton had a plan that he thought would be fool proof. The Secret Commando Force descended upon Little Hades with reckless abandon. However, disaster of epic proportions struck, and the entire force, including General Patton, was completely decimated.

It was later discovered that Satan had been tipped off by a plant. Eventually, it came to light that this plant was none other than that tall beetle, Jake. Peter and his son were devastated at having been fooled by Jake's treachery.

At the Devil's realm, Roman and his evil forces were celebrating the rout of praying mantis soldiers.

"Ah, 'tis a great day, as we've all been drinking and shouting."

Some vegetables and insects were playing poker nearby when one of the insects put his stamp on the operation.

"Ha, Devil-boys. I am full from eating all of those mantises at the cookout."

"Yeah," another said. "Those mantis legs were so delicious roasted!"

"Ditto," said another as he laughed. "God's forces were dealt the Dead Man's Hand, or in this case the Dead Mantis' Claw. Aces and eights."

The whole party roared with laughter, including the newly introduced mosquitoes and fire ants.

One fire ant said, "We will run rampant over those big shot praying mantises. We will cut them down like butter. We will capture many, and no Kung-Fu will stop us. We will tie them to sticks and let the fighters eat them alive!"

"Yes, yes!" Roman was ecstatic. "And we will have plenty of food and drink for the spectator events, just as the Romans of old tortured and killed Christians in the Colosseum."

Of course, the leader of the fire ants, Big Chunk, smiled. "Already, my young fire ants are drooling just thinking about it."

Chapter Ten

S HAWN ROSS' WIFE, KIM, WHO had been confined to a
psychiatric hospital since her husband's death, seemed to
be becoming lucid enough where she was allowed to return
home for a few days. Later, upon switching on the TV, she
heard about the corn that had been killing so many people.
It was this that caused everything to come rushing back to
her... The strange events with Baby Sofia and other things
like the cans of death at the gas station. Ella the so-called
witch tossing plagues from the convertible. Shooting her
and watching her reappear as she ran her over with the
Jeep. Kim needed to talk to someone right away, and it
wouldn't be Mark and Shara, as their baby was suspect in
these paranormal events.

The next day, Kim called Cindy Lue, saying, "Although
my doctors want me to stay in the house, I am going a bit
stir crazy. Can you and Billy meet me at that out of the way
pub for a light lunch and some drinks?"

"Of course," Cindy Lue obliged.

When Billy came home after work, Cindy told him of their plans to meet Kim at the pub.

"Damn, I didn't even know they released her. Boy, I am so glad for her; she's been through hell."

That night Billy and his wife met Kim at a place called The Green Pub, which was covered in Irish banners.

As they all took a seat, Billy said, "Kimmy, order anything. I got you covered."

After ordering, of course, Cindy Lue wasn't going to mention anything about what happened to Shawn. She would let Kim drive the conversation. At first, Kim was speechless as she tried to gather her thoughts into words. Cindy and Billy really didn't know what to say to her.

Finally, Kim said, "I know this sounds unbelievable, but I think Baby Sofia is somehow connected to this poison corn that has been killing people."

Cindy Lue's mouth dropped. Then Kim told them everything about Shawn's family, of the witch trials, of Ella being burned alive and accused of witchcraft. She told them about the hideous man who looked like Satan and Ella trying to kill them on the highway along the cape, referring to it as the Devil's handiwork.

Cindy said, "Kim, maybe you were dreaming this stuff and it just felt real, so you think it really happened. We know you've been under so much stress..."

"Wow. Now you sound like the shrink and all the rest. I think Shawn was murdered by the forces of evil. Why did he use my car hiding in the woods? Because a bright yellow Jeep would stand out too much. I now think he was waiting to kill Baby Sofia and Shara."

"No," Billy said in a bluster, "you can't be serious!"

"Yes. I. Am. Shawn was marked for death, and he knew he was bewitched. He knew he had to run Shara's car off the road and into the river." Kim began sobbing. "Oil cans! We saw them coming alive at the gas station! We watched them horribly kill two men and then try to kill us!"

"Wait, Kim," Cindy said as she put her hand up to slow her friend. "There wasn't any news on the TV in the papers, on the internet, or anything."

"That's just it, Cindy. Satan is behind all of this. After what happened at the gas station suddenly 'never happened'... It's all part of the sick guise of black magic."

Billy stood up. "This is crazy! Where is this gas station?"

"I don't remember the town, but it was on the way back from the Cape. I swear, it was Satan that was driving that huge convertible with Ella in the back seat."

Chapter Eleven

Back with General Ike and the mantis army, all were naturally devastated about the Devil's vengeful killing of hundreds of humans, being poisoned with Spanish flu tainted corn. Ike and his generals brainstormed their next plan of attack. There was a rumor that millions of bed bugs were fanning out to surround some city, but which one? Peter Praying Mantis, now part of the military force, volunteered to sniff around in a covert operation to get as close as possible to Roman's hideout, so they might discover the next target.

Rob Roy was nervous. "Pop, that's dangerous. You could be done in!"

"I know, son, but I must try. Especially since the treachery of Jake the beetle. Don't worry, little mantis, us praying mantises can change our color from green to brown and will blend in nicely, completely camouflaged."

Peter, carrying a pistol in one hand and with an old-time, tiny .45 caliber Tommy gun hanging from his waist, set out to infiltrate the evil compound. Using the stealth of the hunter, Peter saw that two rhubarb guards were patrolling the main gate. Camouflaging himself in the dark of night, he silently crept closer until he cut off the soft head of one of the plants, then dispatched the second with a tactical bowie knife. Inside, he could see onions with hands and feet shooting baskets with a tiny ball. Laughing to himself, Peter thought, *What, the evil army is trying out for the Bulls or the Celtics in between genocides?* But he knew they carried deadly swine flu, so he made sure to be especially careful.

Slipping by them, he soon reached the barracks of the mosquitoes. Looking around, he could see some lounging while others were attacking posters of humans in a training exercise. Then he heard that Satan has given these swarms of deadly mosquitoes the ability to bite infinitely without detection, unlike their brethren above ground, who are swatted at almost immediately. And of course, unlike their average peers, these mosquitoes were tainted with yellow fever.

Inside his ammo belt, slung around his back, Peter retrieved a ball of lethal pesticides. He loaded it quietly into his Tommy gun and peppered the barracks with a hail of poison. Within seconds, every single mosquito lay still, completely annihilated. Peter stood in silence as he considered the level of divine intervention at play; praying mantises have been watching Hollywood movies, like his favorite old gangster movies with stars like Jimmy Cagney, where cops battled robbers with Tommy guns ablaze. Then it dawned on him. *I am Rambo!*

Next, Peter closed in on the wood tick compound, where he sneak up to Roman's office of High Command. It as there that he learned Roman and his wood tick Special Forces guerrilla fighters would be converging on the capitol city, Boston. A legion of at last 40,000 strong. Unfortunately for Peter, his luck had run out. An alert wood tick guard spotted him, and he was quickly surrounded and brought before Roman.

"So, we have a spy?"

"No, I just got lost. That's all."

Big Chunk stepped forward. "Let me have him, Roman. My fire ants will make him talk!"

"No," Roman said, "we can use him as a hostage just as they are holding several lima beans and bed bugs in their prisons."

Chapter Twelve

THE NEXT MORNING, AROUND 2 A.M., several creepy beans slipped in to see Baby Sofia in her bed. They told her of Roman's army and the plan to kill every human on the face of the earth. Sofia cheered as the beans divulged that they too were increasing their numbers in an effort to help strengthen the overall ranks of Satan's master plan. Once the sinister little beans crept away, Sofia was left with her thoughts.

Suddenly jittery, Sofia realized, *ALL humans?! That means my mom and dad! No!*

Aghast, Sofia suddenly realized she had been led down a long dark road that she no longer wished to travel. She must try to stop it now! *Kill mom and dad?! I've been lied to; duped and put under an evil curse.*

Chapter Thirteen

ROMAN THE WOOD TICK SENT a dispatch via black fly to General Ike, demanding release of all beans and bed bugs in exchange for Peter Praying Mantis, otherwise the captive would be brutally tortured to death by the fire ants. General Ike conferred with his diplomats, and the ever-confident Winston Churchill voiced that they were now up against a momentous decision.

"If Peter got into the compound, then I know it can be breached."

Ike thought for a moment, then asked, "What do you have in mind, Winston?"

"I think that the mantis that can get through their defenses is General Martell, named, of course, after the French duke also called 'The Hammer'."

General Charles Martell and all of Ike's inner circle put together a fighting force that would steal their way into Little Hades. It was a small force; something like the U.S. Army Rangers, Navy Seals, or the Marines. Among them were hand-selected mantises, chosen for their skills, rivaling the gunslingers of the old west like Wyatt Earp, Billy the Kid, John Westley Hardin, Henry Plummer, Jesse James, Black Bart, and so many more. Each of these expert marksmen also took famous cowboy actors as their namesakes, such as Gene Autry, Roy Rogers, the Cisco Kid played by Duncan Reinaldo, the Lone Ranger played by Clayton Moore, Tonto played by Jay Silverheels, and many others. These men were idolized by young humans and mantises alike. Of course, the fighting prowess and stealth possessed by every praying mantis typified the Native Americans, such as Pontiac, Sitting Bull, Cochise, Mangas Coloradas, Geronimo, King Philip, Crazy Horse, Roman Nose, the Comanche Quanah Parker, Little Crow, Tecumseh, and many others. Mantises adopted their names as well, hoping to embody their strengths in doing so. These mantises were the top guns of General Martell's invasion forces.

Chapter Fourteen

SATAN, HIS DEMONS, AND HIS minions thought that Ike would try to take Little Hades by force, so they planned to blow them out of the water, so to speak. A band of slimy slugs, headed by Karl Hitler, has been equipped by the Devil with a small neutron bomb that can easily obliterate all attackers.

Roman gloated, saying, "Intel has some telling information on that special task force. It seems they will soon arrive and attempt an attack. They'll be playing right into our checkmate, moved by their own God's hands!"

Big Chunk added, "Then we could raid their grassy fort, and Satan will have millions and billions of human souls. Nothing will stop him and his demons!"

Roman spoke gleefully, "Ha! The humans will be in the dust bin of history and Satan will be master ruler of all!"

Chapter Fifteen

BACK AT MARK AND SHARA'S, the creepy beans once again joined Baby Sofia in her bed. They were all laughing about the plan to nuke General Martell's army of top guns. Then they would race across the above world, blatantly slaughtering every human in their path. Baby Sofia laughed and giggled, happy as a lark. At least, that is the ruse she maintained, her deception completely undetected by the beans. After they left her, Sofia knew she must get word to the mantises, but she was unsure how she could manage.

Chapter Sixteen

A<small>T THE MANTIS FORT, ALL</small> were getting ready, checking their arms and backpacks in a clandestine bivouac against Roman's nest in the Devil's abyss.

General Ike said, "Charles, I trust all operations are able and ready to go?"

"Without a doubt, General Ike. With out plan, logistics, some luck, and the Almighty, we can be assured that the day will be ours and the Axis of Evil will be obliterated."

Chapter Seventeen

A<small>T</small> M<small>ARK</small> <small>AND</small> S<small>HARA'S</small> <small>AGAIN</small>, the couple brought Sofia outside to enjoy the warm July day, hoping she might enjoy a little bask in the sun. Then Shara brought out iced teas for herself and Mark as well as a cold bottle of milk for Sofia. After a little while, Mark walked over with a praying mantis in his hand.

"Look, Shara! A praying mantis!"

Shara smiled. "I haven't seen one in a dog's age. Show it to Sofia."

As Sofia looked, Mark said, "You know, Shara, I read an article a while back about this bug. They are called the Kung-Fu fighters of the insect world."

Shara was taken aback. "Wow, no kidding. Can they fly?"

"Only the males. They can also change colors."

Suddenly Sofia stood up, looking intensely at the bug.

Shara laughed. "I think Sofia might have a new friend."

Mark placed it in Sofia's open hand for her to hold,

where it sat for a moment before floating off to a nearby apple tree.

"Well," Mark said, "at least she got the thrill of being close to nature."

Then the next door neighbor came over. Johnny, a boy of about twelve, often helped Mark with yard work. Shara went into the house, knowing Mark was close by to Sofia's playpen. As Mark and Johnny busied themselves in conversation, the mantis flew back onto the rail of the playpen.

Sofia said softly, "Mantis can you help me?"

The mantis dude replied, "Yes, I think I might be able to help you, little girl. I am Theodore."

Sofia smiled broadly.

Theodore continued, "I know you need help."

"How would you know that?"

"God works in strange ways."

"Yes, Theodore, I do need help. I know that I have been bewitched with witchcraft, but now I want to fight back and destroy it." After pausing a moment, she quickly added, "I found out through the evil beans that Roman Wood Tick's forces are going to set of a neutron bomb when General Martell goes into Little Hades. It's going to happen in one day. Can you please help me?"

"Physically, I would, Sofia, but I got into a scrape with a couple of locusts a while back and injured two of my six legs. Actually, that's why I hang around in your yard. I have a friend that I think may be able to help you. He's my bosom buddy, Pedro, the inch worm."

Sofia cried out, "An inch worm!"

"Yes, Pedro can catch wind currents and float to the mantis' fort."

Sofia was delighted. "So, will – Oh wait! There he is hanging from a leaf!"

Theodore quickly filled him in on the crisis. Pedro told Sofia he would do his best as long as there were strong breezes to carry him.

Chapter Eighteen

$\mathcal{B}$ACK AT ROMAN'S, THE SLUGS were working to bring the neutron bomb to blow General Martell to smithereens.

Roman chuckled, "In a few hours, the mantis fort will be ours, and we will send trillions and trillions of diseased insects and vegetables across the globe to unleash deadly pandemics and kill the humans!"

Chapter Nineteen

Pedro caught a light breeze, which took him closer to the main fort, but as it was July the wind sometimes barely stirred. However, so tiny, so insignificant, and so light, Pedro somehow got within a few miles of the fort before the wind seemed to shut down completely. The stillness of the air created a deafening silence. Knowing only 55 minutes remained before the bomb would detonate, Pedro scrambled to find a way to beat the clock.

Up ahead, Pedro could see a kaleidoscope of monarch butterflies fluttering about. He tried to climb up a nearby tree so that they might see him, but he knew he wouldn't make it in time. Suddenly, he was confronted by a dragonfly.\

Oh no! Pedro thought. *This is my end!*

The dragonfly said, "Do not fret, little one, I have been sent by the glorious heavenly force that reverberates throughout all sweet nectar, soft rose petals, and shining rays. I am Gabriel, and I will fly you, little inch worm, to the monarch butterflies."

"Wow." Pedro was spellbound.

"Latch onto a wing and we will be off."

Before long Pedro found himself aboard with the butterflies, led by Jasper, who reached General Ike in record time. The general then sent a small unit of Army Rangers and Navy Seals down into Little Hades, where, in an unprecedented sneak attack, they neutralized the bomb. The mantis army followed close behind them, taking out Roman, Big Chunk, and most of Roman's vile forces, including that wretched traitor, Jake the beetle.

Later that night, Pedro the inch worm was feted at a victor banquet. Kudos were given to the butterflies, Theodore the praying mantis, Gabriel the dragonfly, and, of course, Baby Sofia. Although it was a significant victory, General Ike knew that Satan would try another of the filthy tricks he kept up his sleeve, bringing about the worst from his filthy cesspool of malignant demons and vile monsters because he was truly the darkest epitome of an Anti-God. The Ruler of Hell. The Prince of Darkness. He will surely unleash his wrath because of what has happened. Satan and his demons now will want to go after Sofia, which renounced the darkness and saw the goodness and salvation of God in an effort to fight against him.

Of course, God was not going to be outfoxed as the chess game intensified. Baby Sofia was happy and relieved that Pedro the inch worm had been able to wand the praying mantises, but something told her that not everything was right.

Chapter Twenty

MARK ARRIVED BACK AT THE job site and joined his brother, Billy, saying, "I think we only have a week or two left here. The renovations have gone rather smoothly."

"Yeah." Billy quipped, "Cindy Lue's aunt is letting us use her summer cottage in Dennis on the Cape for a week when I get laid off. You and Shara and the baby are welcome to join us."

"Sounds good. I'm sure Shara's going to be on board with that."

The next two weeks passed quickly. Billy pulled into Mark's driveway in his classic '69 Camaro. Mark was washing his fairly new Chevy Silverado pickup.

"Thought I would swing by. Cindy Lue wants to know if Shara can bring her margarita recipe."

"Oh, without a doubt!" Mark smiles. "Should I grab the steak tips are Roscoe's Market in town?"

"Yeah, I would. We know his are always the best. Plus,

I'm sure they will be cheaper than down the Cape." Billy emphasized, "Everything else, we got. Just bring your Bud Lights. I got my Millers and some good new brews that seem to pop up every month."

As he got back into his red Camaro, Billy nodded to the truck, "Say, how's your baby running?"

"Great, but I think I've got an exhaust leak. I'll take care of it when we get back."

Chapter Twenty-One

THE FOLLOWING SUNDAY MORNING THE two couples and Baby Sofia were en route to the Cape.

Mark was following Billy's Car when Shara commented, "Isn't this great, hon? I know Sofia is loving it."

After considerable time, they pulled alongside the canal to stretch their legs and let Sofia look at the water. Suddenly, Mark saw wood ticks climbing up her leg.

"Damn!" Mark yelled, picking her up and brushing them off.

Billy walked over. "Yeah, they thrive in this saw grass."

They quickly left the edge of the canal and soon pulled up to the cottage.

"Nice place," Mark remarked. "Pretty much secluded."

"Yup, Aunt Helen and Uncle Joe bought this place years ago, but since his passing she seldom comes down here."

Unloading their vehicles, they lit a campfire to cook a few hamburgers and hotdogs. Sitting around and shooting the breeze, Cindy Lue noticed a small patch on the side of the house with corn growing.

Billy said, "I never knew that they made a corn field."

Shara walked over. "Yeah, but I wouldn't eat it. Ever since that out break a while back, you just never know."

Mark responded, "I know, but the corn around Rockville and Park City was the problem, not the Cape."

Shara blinked her black eyes. "I know, hon, but would you eat it?"

Cindy Lue and Billy both mirrored her concern, agreeing it looked delicious but shouldn't be risked.

That night around 2a.m., Cindy Lue heard scratching. She shook Billy awake.

"Do you hear that?"

"Hear what?"

"Like something scratching?"

"Not really, but I thought I heard something, maybe. Probably just a raccoon or something looking for food."

"Hon, put your pants on and take a look."

"Oh, woman, every time you hear a noise in the night you think it's some spook," Billy said as he walked into the kitchen, checking around and listening. Suddenly a profile of someone in the living room startled him. Then Mark walked over.

"Billy, what are you doing?"

"Cindy said she heard something."

Mark nodded, "So did Shara. I think it was an animal snooping around."

"Ditto," Billy breathed. "Let's go back to bed."

Billy climbed back into bed beside his wife, who looked at him expectantly.

"Well?"

"Mark and I check it out. We think it was probably just some animal poking around."

Then Billy put his hand under her negligee. "Say, why don't we make the best of this interruption?"

"No, Billy, knock it off now. I'm tired."

"But Sweet-cheeks, I'm not."

Cindy threw the bed covering over her head. "Good night, husband!"

Chapter Twenty-Two

IN THE MORNING, CINDY LUE and Shara wanted to go into town to buy some summer wares and check out the latest swimwear. Shara drove them in the pickup. The men stayed behind, preferring not to spend their day shopping. Mark opened up his light jacket, showing his brother a .32 snugly fitted into his shoulder holster.

"Yeah, I figured you would pack."

Mark's phone rang; it was Shara letting him know they picked up a watermelon and would be home soon. Before long, the girls drove up in the gunmetal Silverado.

Shara shared, "It was a fine shopping trip until a car seemed to be following us a bit too close."

"Yeah," Cindy Lue agreed, "Two guys in a Honda Civic."

Mark blinked. "Was it a faded gray one with a door that didn't match?"

"I didn't notice the door," Shara said, "but it was gray."

"They drove by here a couple of hours ago."

Chapter Twenty-Three

AFTER EVERYONE HAD A SMALL casserole that Cindy made, they all played gin rummy until about 11:30p.m. when they decided to finally turn in. Billy was checking out Cindy Lue's buys from the shopping trip when he came across a tasseled pair of panties.

Billy's mouth twitched up at the corners as he said, "Hey, sexy girl. Love these panties." He held them up for emphasis.

Cindy Lue smiled. "Honey, I'll wear them when we get home, but right now it's my turn in the shower.

Billy crawled into bed to wait for her. Cindy knew exactly what was on his mind as he smirked up at her.

"No way, Billy Boy; the walls are paper thin."

He embraced her.

"No, Billy. Like I said, hold off until we know they're asleep."

"Oh, Cindy, they're probably getting into it themselves…"

"No, hubby. Control yourself."

"OK, OK…. I just want to latch onto your nipples for a couple hours…"

"Ha, ha. You're a riot."

Billy walked his fingers down the hard plane of her belly, moving lower.

"Honey, come on now. I know you can control yourself. And besides you might wake up Sofia."

"OK, honey, if you say so. But can't I just put my chest into your sweet breasts?"

"Billy, I know making love in old' Cape Cod is exhilarating, but wait a little while until we're sure they're asleep."

"OK, Sweetie, but you know I am hornier than a half-fucked fox."

Cindy threw her pillow at him laughing.

In the morning, Shara made everyone a sunshine breakfast. Once finished, Mark and Shara left to get some wine coolers for later. Billy and Cindy Lue were sitting at the kitchen table when Cindy spoke.

"You know, Billy, I was kind of reluctant to go on this trip because of what Kim was telling us about Sofia and how she said she was plotting to kill her husband."

"I know, me too. Saying oil cans came alive, killing two gas station attendants. Some Ella from the 17th century who was burned for witchcraft was throwing plagues from a huge, open convertible…"

"I think unfortunately it is just the twisted mind of a wife who couldn't cope with the death of her husband. She was delusional."

"Could be, Hon."

"I am sorry she thinks it's all true. I am. Watching Sofia closely, she looks like any normal four-year-old."

"I agree, Babes. Then remember she said Satan was driving the convertible? Poor Kim!"

Chapter Twenty-Four

THAT NIGHT AS EVERYONE SETTLED into bed around 12:30a.m., a python slithered into a small vent and through the crawl space under the cottage. Somehow making its way through the insulation, it prowled around and slid in through a partially open door to Mark and Shara's bedroom. From there, it headed for the playpen where Sofia was sleeping. The snake inadvertently brushed against one of Sofia's rattles, making enough noise that Shara looked over and screamed bloody murder. Mark jumped up, grabbing his .32 and shooting it, but the snake continued to advance. When Billy head the outcry from the other room, he came in and looked on in horror. Without thinking, he grabbed his machete and chopped the beast's head off.

Everyone met in the kitchen to catch their breath and try to calm their pounding hearts. Mark was still stunned for another moment before he was able to speak.

"The .32 seemed to have no effect."

"Yeah," Billy said, flushed just as white as the rest. "Low caliber."

Shara held the baby tight.

"It seemed like the snake was going right for Sofia," she said as perspiration still ran down her face.

"I don't know..." Mark could hardly get the words out.

Shara kept the baby pressed close to her bosom as she said, "Let's get out of here. I could never spend another night after that."

Cindy Lue considered. "I think someone dumped a pet snake, probably after it got too big."

"Could be," Mark said. "There are a lot of small ponds around here. All fresh water."

When dawn arrived, Billy and Mark investigated how the snake was able to get in.

"How old is this cottage?" Mark asked.

Billy thought for a minute. "I think it was built in the 1930's? My uncle Joe is only the second owner."

Between the two of them, they were able to figure out how the snake had likely gotten in, and they replaced the old, rotted board to prevent any further intrusions. Only four days remained in their planned stay before another party would be staying there in the coming week.

Although Shara wanted to go home immediately, everyone convinced her to stay by deciding that each person would rotate and keep guard through the wee hours of the morning. Gladly, nothing happened.

Finally, with only one day left, they all decided to throw a big cookout and have a pig roast. Besides the beer and the coolers, they cracked open a bottle of champagne. In the midst of their partying, the same Honda Civic drove slowly by. Billy saw Mark head for his pickup.

"What's up, Mark?"

"I'm going to follow that sucker and find out why they've been so damn nosy."

"Be careful. You don't know who they are."

"I'll be careful. But I'm also glad that I traded in my .32 for the Glock .99mm. Watch the girls, Billy."

Chapter Twenty-Five

MARK CAUGHT UP TO THEM on the main highway, then laid back. Next, he saw them take a dirt road off to the side. He followed them, hopefully undetected. Suddenly, the road narrowed considerably and Mark got a sinking feeling in his stomach. Up ahead he could see a small house set back from the road. Cautiously, he pulled over to the side, then planned that he would approach from the side through the woods. He put his hand on his holstered gun, reassuring himself, as he scanned for any possible danger.

After walking only a short distance, the woods opened up into a field where an elderly woman was sitting at a table with a sign that read "Onions For Sale". Mark immediately though the scene didn't look right. The woman smiled.

"Sir, would you like some Vidalia onions from Georgia?"

Mark was trying to make sense of the bizarre woman before him, seated at a table in the middle of nowhere.

"Oh, I got lost. I'm sorry. I'll just go back the way I came."

"But, sir, these sweet Vidalia onions are a great buy."

"Er, no thanks."

He knew he had to get out of there quickly. Pushing back to his pickup, he knew that he would have to scrap his plans to spy on the house for now.

Back at the cottage, Mark spewed out the strange encounter. Billy was completely perplexed.

"A woman in the woods, selling onions?" he asked.

"Yeah," Mark replied, "it was like walking through the woods when you come up to an ice cream stand."

Billy paced in a circle, as he said, "Maybe I'll take a ride and check out that house. It's probably connected to the kinky woman."

"Brother," Mark chimed in, "maybe we should just leave like we plan to do in the morning and get back to Rockville and Park City. Our wives are still jumpy about that snake. We don't want to add fuel to the fire with this."

"I guess you're right," Billy agreed.

Chapter Twenty-Six

THE FOLLOWING MORNING, THEY ALL packed up and started on their way home from the Cape. Before leaving, they decided to make a quick stop at Uncle Frosty's ice cream stand. Parking side by side, they all got their cones and sat together on one of the many benches. Soon, the rumble of a Dodge Challenger shook the air as it pulled in. Of course, Billy had to check it out. Both men were then commenting on the Challenger and Billy's Camaro as well.

Cindy Lue laughed, "Billy's in his glory now. Speed is in his veins."

Everybody chuckled. Mark went back up to the stand to get more napkins for Sofia, as she was, quite happily, covered in chocolate ice cream. Just as he was pulling napkins from their holder, a huge convertible pulled in. Mark overheard another customer mention to his wife that it was a 1957 Imperial. Suddenly, he remembered it was the same car from the coffee shop a few years back when he went with Shawn Ross to get iced coffees for their wives in Harwich.

It all came back to him in that moment. Jay Leno owns a '57 Imperial. Then, looking over to the open convertible, he saw the same ugly guy behind the wheel. This time, a boy of about twelve was with him, not the young girl like before. Mark returned with the napkins to wipe the baby's face.

Nodding to his brother, he said, "Billy, you love cars. You should check out that 1957 Imperial on the other side. Talk about enormous cars of the 50's!"

Billy motioned to Cindy Lue and they walked over together. Cindy watched as Billy seemed to turn pale.

"Hon, what's wrong?"

"Remember Kim telling us about the chase? About an open convertible with an ugly man wearing a red bandana?"

It was at that moment they saw the car. Cindy looked scared.

"But she said there was a young girl..."

"So what?", Mark questioned, "He changed passengers."

Billy held out a hand to signal to Mark to hold back.

"I'm going to confront the driver."

Without looking suspicious, he nonchalantly drifted over to the car.

"Wow!" Billy espoused, "What a classic! Someone said it's a 1957 Imperial?"

The ugly man looked up, completely ignoring Billy, as he said, "Jimmy, let's go." With that, he drove off.

Cindy watched the entire interaction. "What a jerk!"

Billy spewed out, "Maryland plates. When we get back, I'll ask Kim about the plate if she remembers."

Chapter Twenty-Seven

BACK UNDERNEATH THE GARDEN IN Rockville, a new leader emerged to replace Roman after he was killed in Little Hades. Pontius Pilate was a hefty wood tick and was accompanied by the new leader of the fire ants, Ivan the Terrible.

"My condolences about Big Chunk," Pontius began. "He was an exceptional killer, well-versed in the proper way to dispatch mantises with the slowest and most deliberate and excruciating tortures."

"Yes, Big Chunk attended Satan's School of Horror, where he and his demons taught the fine points of ripping, gouging, and lopping limbs off. Yes, he will be sorely missed."

Ivan then called Pontius over to a small table.

"The mantises control Little Hades for now, but I have a plan to drive them out."

"What's the plan then?" Pontius was eager.

Ivan stoked his own ego, saying, "We have recruited Dirty Thelma, the head of the black widow spiders, and she will lead a thousand of her spider army loaded with smallpox to annihilate General Ike's army of mantises."

Pontius looked skeptical. "Why do you think this plan will work when others have failed?"

"Well, for one, Dirty Thelma's army will drop from the air in parachutes made from webs. I am sure you have heard about how the Japanese made a surprise attack on the humans on December 7, 1941, in Hawaii?"

"Yeah, so what about it?"

"It's the same idea, Pontius. The mantises will be overrun from the air as Dirty Thelma's surprise attack will bring about a great victory for Satan."

Ivan was beaming as he said, "Already my sharp mouth is watering."

Chapter Twenty-Eight

BACK WITH THE HUMANS, MARK and Shara, along with Baby Sofia, returned to their home. However, Billy and Cindy Lue wanted to talk to Kim sooner rather than later. Cindy called her on the phone, but her brother Kevin answered, telling her that Kim kind of went off the rails and is back in the hospital for more treatment.

At Mark and Shara's house, Mark put Sofia in the playpen while he was catching up on the mail. Sofia then spotted Pedro, who slowly dropped down.

"Hi, little girl. Do you remember me? I'm Pedro."

"Yes, I know who you are, and I'm grateful that you saved the mantis fort."

"Thank you, Sofia. I was only doing God's work. However, it has come to me that the vile black widow spiders, led by Dirty Thelma, are planning to attack the mantis fort as we speak,"

"How do you know that?"

"A wayward grasshopper somehow found out and passed the news on to me."

Sofia panicked. "I must find a way to warn General Ike!"

"Unfortunately, that's not all I heard. Apparently, Satan has put a target on you as well."

Sofia gasped, "Me?!"

"It was said that you tipped of the mantises through me and touted them."

Sofia now became belligerent. "And I would do it 100 times more!!"

"It's okay, my pretty girl. Gabriel the dragonfly is going to set up a perimeter around your playpen with specialized dragonfly commandos, who are time-tested in every possible scenario. Also, I wanted to let you know that I no longer need to rely on the wind, for in two days I will turn into a moth, and I'll be able to fly to General Ike myself!"

Sofia was beyond joyful.

In the mantis green camp, General Ike knew that his army was severely decimated when General Patton and his command were taken out. Today he would gather his special corps of mantises that took on the identities of various cowboys and Native Americans, who would fight beside the regular army.

Ike put them through intensive training to prepare for any additional demonic attacks. Little did he know, it couldn't come any sooner, when Pedro, now a moth, told him of how Pontius Pilate and Ivan the Terrible were planning a sneak attack led by Dirty Thelma and her black widow spiders.

Ike sent three mantises as scouts to try to discover

more about Pilate's plans. Jay Silverheels, Crazy Horse, and Cochise got into the compound of the wood ticks' hideout and were shocked at what they saw, Hundreds of black widow spiders were constructing parachutes out of their webs. They were going to lead an aerial assault to slaughter the mantises. Returning back, the scouts told General Ike of their information. Now Ike had to think of a way to neutralize the spiders. Given that the enemy force held a thousand or more deadly black widows, it was a daunting task.

Pedro soon returned to Sofia in the playpen. Fluttering over, he said, "General Ike is trying to come up with a weapon to take the spiders down."

Then all Sofia could visualize was the spiders overwhelming the mantis army and it froze her very blood.

Shara walked over as Pedro flew to the apple tree.

"How's my precious little girl?"

Mark joined them, saying, "Hon, why is your finger in your mouth?"

"Oh, I am chewing bubble gum, and it's stuck in my teeth."

Mark laughed, "Keep working on it, Hon!" as they sat down in their lawn chairs.

Pedro flew back to the playpen, looking at Sofia as he said, "You look deep in thought."

Sofia nodded. "Yes, I am. I was thinking… Do you think that General Ike could attack the spiders with bubble gum?"

Pedro was mystified. "Bubblegum?" he asked. "I don't follow you, little girl."

"Well, Pedro, if somehow General Ike could make it wet and sticky and use it in the mantises' armaments…"

Pedro fluttered his wings. "You might be on to something, Sofia."

Sofia smiled. "It's food for thought."

"Where would they get the bubble gum? That's in the human domain."

"Pedro," Sofia asked, "can you fly to General Ike to see what he says?"

"I would if I could, but my lifespan is only 30 days, and it's nearing the end. However, I think Gabriel will go for us. He's a true patriot and, as you know, a protector."

Following a brief conversation between human, moth, and dragonfly, Gabriel set out with a rather outrageous plan to decimate Dirty Thelma and her black widow spiders, surrogates of the devil. At the grass fort, Gabriel ran Sofia's idea by General Ike and his team. While they all agreed it had merit, they were unsure how they would be able to get a hold of any themselves. Winston Churchill stepped forward.

"There are many things that go into bubble gum which I am not acquainted with; however, there is one ingredient I do know about called beetroot. The taproot portion of a beet plant. If we could come up with the other ingredients to make it sticky, we could very well have our ace in the hole."

The Roosevelt cousins were on board with the plan. Peter Mantis, now an adviser to Ike, shared his thoughts.

"Mantises, I know that Albert Einstein is getting up there in age, his wings turning gray. However, I would think he could come up with the other ingredients to make bubble gum."

Ike mirrored Peter's assertion. "I'll have an audience with the old mantis chap."

In the meantime, Ike's high command was forming

ranks of mantis sharp shooters with many having adopted the names of famous gunslingers, like Billy the Kid, Wild Bill Hickock, and Annie Oakley with her sharpshooting husband, Frank Butler. Those who had taken names of famous actors like Gene Autry, Duncan Renaldo, Clayton Moore, and Clint Eastwood joined ranks with others who adopted the identities of the strongest Native American warriors, like Pontiac, Red Cloud, and Geronimo.

Although the mantis scouts discovered how Pontius Pilate and Ivan the Terrible planned to use the black widows in Satan's war on mankind's souls, they still did not know that, on Satan's directive, Pilate unleashed millions more fire ants to join the battle. Already they were making their way up from the bowels of the vegetable garden, preparing for the assault. Joining them would be a 200-dog-face limit of rhubarb special forces.

Chapter Twenty-Nine

I N WHAT COULD ONLY BE called warp speed, Einstein came up with a recipe for bubble gum. General Ike added more sharpshooters to the ranks, concealing them in foxholes for when Thelma's forces took to the sky. Rounds from a variety of weapons including long rifles, Tommy guns, AK 47's, shotguns and more were readied. Instead of the regular gunpowder, the rounds consisted of the sticky solution that would pauperize Dirty Thelma's smallpox-laced spiders and wreak havoc on the rest of Pilate's forces.

The die was cast. As the sharpshooters would be taking down the black widows, General Ike's main force would attack in a pincer formation; hopefully, squeezing the enemy in all directions. Now being rather confident, the bulk of the army moved out on a two-day march, where they were confronted by millions of fire ants emerging from a deep hole. Some pulled and pushed large cannons on wheels. What came next could have been a quirk or divine intervention. Suddenly the sky opened up with a gale force deluge, cracking thunder and bolts of lighting, as torrential rain flooded the basin, wiping out all of the fire ants. As quickly as it began, the weather cleared.

From the skies, Dirty Thelma's spiders began to parachute down to earth, where the snipers opened fire in a blitzing volley of bubble gum dis-chargers. As he was blasting spiders, Billy the Kid remarked that it was just like a turkey shoot. Unfortunately, a rhubarb dog-face soldier shot Wild Bill Hickock in the back, killing him. Tom Mix was driving a small tank when it hit a big rock and flipped, killing him as well. For the most part, the bubble gum finished the black widows. Cochise then spotted Thelma with her massive red hourglass marking on her abdomen. She was attempting to escape when he shouted to her.

"Dirty Thelma, this round of Double Bubble is for you!!"

With that, she suffocated in the gooey gum.

General Ike's forces then took out the dog-face rhubarb forces and won the day. Satan was licking his chops, so to speak, knowing there would soon be another day for his wrath!

Chapter Thirty

IT WAS THE END OF August when Mark and Shara took Sofia to a dog park so she could see all the canines. While her parents were talking to a man about his Great Dane, Gabriel flew down and landed on her stroller. Sofia was elated.

"Gabriel! How are you?"

"I am great, little child. I have both sad news and happy news for you. Pedro the moth has passed; his contribution is now legend."

"Yes," Sofia said as she wiped away a tear.

Gabriel smiled. "I have been sent by General Ike to ask you to host a wedding in your bedroom."

Sofia was shocked. "In my bedroom!"

"Well, Sofia, it seems that Peter Mantis is getting married again, and he knows you came up with the bubble gum plan to take down Dirty Thelma, so he wants to honor you by having the rites in your bedroom."

"Oh, yes, yes! Thank you, thank you. That would be double awesome!"

"OK, sweet girl, I'll send word to General Ike and Peter. The wedding is to be held on August 31st."

Chapter Thirty-One

THE MORNING OF THE 31ST, Peter and his bride-to-be, Julia, made the trip to Park City. Of course, this whole scenario occurred under the loving hands of God in Heaven. Seats were arranged for the more than one hundred guests ranging from praying mantises to crickets to dragonflies. Butterflies, ladybugs, the rosy maple moth, inch worms – more types of insects than could be counted.

The Reverend Chester Grasshopper would be officiating the ceremony. Peter Mantis' best man was to be the mantis general, Charles Martell. The bridal party consisted of Julia's two sisters and her best friend and maid of honor, Honey-cup Bumblebee. As Peter was getting ready for his big day, he and Rob Roy were shining their wings when he looked over at his son.

"Rob Roy, why do you look so sad?"

"Pop," Rob Roy looked stressed, "is Julia going to eat you too?"

"No, son, I'll be fine," he chuckled.

Before the ceremony began, General Ike announced that he would like to make a presentation.

"Insects, bugs, if you will. Thank you for coming to the wedding of Peter and Julia. As you know, Peter lost his first wife from a virus and has a wonderful son, Rob Roy. Peter wanted to honor the human, Sofia, for her role in the great bubble gum plan, giving the forces of good a giant step against Satan's evil doctrine. With that, I turn it over to Reverend Chester."

On the walls, the crickets were chirping and Rufus the beetle was playing the organ. Peter walked down the aisle along with General Martell. Next, Julia was escorted by her father, "Take No Prisoners" Mantis. Then all the wedding participants stood up front. The Reverend Grasshopper began.

"Dearly beloved, we are here to join together Peter and Julia in holy matrimony. Peter, will you protect Julia from predatory insects and love her as long as you shall live?"

"I will."

"And you, Julia, Will you keep Peter well and, if needed, mend any or all of his six claw-legs?"

"I will."

General Martell gave Peter the ring, Peter then slid it onto Julia's front claw.

"Now you may kiss the bride!"

At once the crowd of insects erupted in cheers, some offering Sofia praise for her part as well.

Sofia tried to downplay it, saying, "Really I saw my mother chewing it and that's how I got the idea." She doubted anyone heard her though,

Just before the celebrations broke up, General Ike presented Sofia with a tiny, gold-wrapped box, with a sword and a Christian cross and an even tinier piece of bubble gum inside.

"Sofia, on behalf of the insects that joined our crusade against Lucifer and his seven fallen angels, we are grateful.

Chapter Thirty-Two

THE NEXT MORNING, SHARA WENT to get Sofia to change and feed her.

"Honey-gal, rise and shine!" she said as she brought her into the kitchen.

Mark was finishing his coffee as they entered.

"It must feel good that the union hall called you for a job," she said.

"Yeah, definitely. And I was talking to Billy last night on the cell. He said that he and Lyla Cody also got the call for the job over in Pacerville."

"That's great," Shara smiled. "Say, Hon, before you go, will you go get Sofia's favorite rattle in her bed?"

"Sure."

At the Martin house everything is ordinary. Outside everything is ordinary. What happened never happened. Things are whey they're supposed to be because that's the way God wants it to be. However, as Mark went to Sofia's bed to grab her rattle, the morning sun shone through the window, reflecting off of the gold paper on the tiny box. Mark was mystified. What could it be? How did it get there? Picking it up, he brought it to Shara.

"Hon, I saw this on the floor. Is it something you bought?"

Shara looked dumbfounded, saying, "A tiny box with a ribbon with a sword and a cross??"

"You mean you never say it before?" Mark asked.

"No never."

Mark urged her to open the ribbon to see what the tiny box held. Shara opened it up, finding a tiny piece of bubble gum. Shara's eyes widened.

"Bubblegum?! What the heck!"

Mark laughed, "It must have been sent by the bubble gum company because you're always buying the stuff."

"Oh, come on, Mark! That's crazy. And a Christian cross and sword? It doesn't make sense."

"Well, Babes, I've got to get going. I don't want to be late on the first day on the job." He paused before adding, "You know everything around here is do damn ordinary, this is mind-boggling."

As Shara kept reflecting on what it could be, Mark jumped in his pickup and headed for the job.

Sofia, in the highchair, was fascinated by the bright gold paper on the box. However, Shara saw her give a great big smile as she stared at it, Then Shara looked down to the box and, for some unknown reason, she had a smile as well.

Printed in the United States
by Baker & Taylor Publisher Services